THE
CIVIL WAR

The Child's World

Published by The Child's World®
1980 Lookout Drive • Mankato, MN 56003-1705
800-599-READ • www.childsworld.com

ACKNOWLEDGMENTS
The Child's World®: Mary Berendes, Publishing Director
Red Line Editorial: Editorial direction
The Design Lab: Design
Amnet: Production
Content Consultant: Barbara Gannon, Assistant Professor of
History, University of Central Florida

Photographs ©: Library of Congress, cover, 6, 9, 11, 12, 15, 17
(top), 20, 22, 23, 25, 29; The Design Lab, 5; Northwind/AP
Images, 10; Corbis, 17 (bottom), 18; Bettmann/Corbis, 26

Design elements: Shutterstock Images

ISBN 9781631437069
LCCN 2014945393

Printed in the United States of America
Mankato, MN
November, 2014
PA02243

ABOUT THE AUTHOR

Thomas K. Adamson has written dozens of nonfiction books for kids on sports, space, history, math, and more. He lives in Sioux Falls, South Dakota, with his wife and two sons. He enjoys sports, card games, and reading and playing ball with his sons.

TABLE OF CONTENTS

CHAPTER ONE

THE BATTLE OF GETTYSBURG

★ ★ ★

The Northern and Southern states had been fighting a brutal civil war for a little more than two years. The Northern soldiers were considered part of the Union. The Southerners were called Confederates. Thousands of soldiers from both sides now met near Gettysburg, Pennsylvania, on July 1, 1863. The Southern army had recently invaded Northern territory. The North needed to force it back.

The battle raged into a second day. Union Sergeant Alfred Carpenter was with the First Minnesota **Infantry**. They were on a hill called Cemetery Ridge. The gunfire was a continuous roar. Smoke rose from the guns and **artillery**. Carpenter could tell what was going on only by sound.

Canada

Minnesota

Maine

Vermont

Oregon

Wisconsin

New
Hampshire

United States

Michigan

New York

Massachusetts

Connecticut

Rhode Island

Nevada

Iowa

Pennsylvania

fornia

Illinois

Indiana

Ohio

New Jersey

Delaware

Maryland

Kansas

Missouri

West
Virginia

Virginia

Kentucky

North Carolina

Arkansas

Tennessee

South
Carolina

Mississippi

Georgia

Texas

Alabama

Louisiana

Florida

Mexico

The Bahamas

N

NW

NE

E

W

SW

SE

S

MAP KEY

★ ★ ★

Union States

Confederate
States

Border States

5

A monument to the First Minnesota Infantry stands near Gettysburg, Pennsylvania.

Approximately 1,600 Confederate soldiers marched toward Carpenter and his fellow Union soldiers. The First Minnesota was outnumbered. The Confederates were about to capture the Union's cannons. Union General Winfield Scott Hancock had to buy just a little time until help arrived. He ordered the First Minnesota to charge the Confederates.

The Minnesotans did not hesitate. All 262 men poured down the hill. Bullets whistled past Carpenter. Friends he had trained and fought with were hit. No one stopped. They would mourn their fallen friends later.

The First Minnesota drove the Confederates back. Hancock got the time he needed to bring up reserves. The cost was high: 215 of the 262 men in the First Minnesota were killed or wounded in the charge. Carpenter was one of the few who survived, and he was badly wounded.

This brave charge was part of one of the Civil War's major battles. And the battle may have turned the tide of the whole war.

ANOTHER VIEW

Imagine you are an officer in charge of nearly 300 men. Many of them are your friends. But in order to win the battle you need to order them to make a dangerous charge. Many of them will die. How do you feel ordering men you know so well to their deaths?

CHAPTER TWO

CAUSES OF THE WAR

★ ★ ★

Throughout the early 1800s, tensions between the North and South had been rising. The two halves of the country were developing different economies. The South's warm climate was perfect for cotton. People worked on large farms called **plantations**. In the North, more people worked in factories than in the South.

Plantation owners in the South used slaves to work the fields. They believed that without slavery, the plantations would not make a profit. Some people in the North wanted to **abolish** slavery. Many did not want it to expand into the west. The North thought the national government should decide whether slavery should be allowed to expand to other places. The South thought the federal government

Slaves work in the fields on a plantation in South Carolina in 1862.

should not be involved with deciding where slavery should be allowed.

Enslaved Africans had been kidnapped and brought to America against their will. Slaves were not given a say because they were legally the property of their white owners, as were their children. They were forced to work for no pay. For most slaves, life was brutal and hopeless. Many were beaten by their owners for not working hard enough. Sometimes slaves were not given enough food for all that hard work.

Slave and free states and territories in 1857

HARPERS FERRY RAID

Abolitionist John Brown was ready to do anything to get rid of slavery. In 1859, Brown and 21 men raided an **armory** at Harpers Ferry, Virginia. This armory had thousands of guns. Brown thought slaves would join him and fight against slave owners. But none did. U.S. soldiers went to Harpers Ferry to stop Brown. Several died in the fight. Brown was captured. He was executed a few weeks later. This event brought more attention to the slavery issue.

Slaves could be sold to other slave owners at any time. This often separated family members. Some slaves risked their lives to escape and reunite with their families.

Plantation owners became wealthy because the labor was free. If slavery was abolished, the South's way of life would completely change.

The United States was expanding quickly to the west. Western territories were being added as new states. The North and South argued whether the territories should be slave states or free states.

Congress agreed to the Missouri Compromise in 1820. The compromise admitted Missouri and Maine as new states. Slavery would be allowed in Missouri but not in Maine. In addition, slavery would not be allowed in new land west of Missouri's southern border. The compromise and other

Abraham Lincoln

measures like it eased tensions for a while but did not solve the root problem.

There were many disputes over expanding slavery in the 1850s. Northerners supported Abraham Lincoln when he ran for president In 1860. The South did not want Lincoln to win. Southerners feared that he would abolish slavery.

Lincoln won a close election. Not a single Southern state supported him. A few weeks later South Carolina **seceded** from the Union. Within six weeks, six other states left the Union. They wanted to maintain their way of life. They together formed the Confederate States of America. They chose their own president, Jefferson Davis, and created a government at Richmond, Virginia.

Union forces surrendered Fort Sumter on April 13, 1861, after heavy bombardment.

The Confederacy began taking over military forts in the South. Fort Sumter, South Carolina, remained under Union control. In early 1861, more than 6,000 Confederates surrounded it.

Early on April 12, approximately 50 Confederate cannons fired on the fort from four different directions. The walls of Fort Sumter crumbled. The next day, fires broke out in the fort. Union troops were forced to surrender.

President Lincoln called for volunteers to enlist in the military. The Confederacy also called for new soldiers. Virginia, North Carolina, Arkansas, and Tennessee joined the Confederacy. The war had begun.

ANOTHER VIEW

If you were a young man living in a **Northern state** and had relatives who lived in a **Southern state**, how would you feel about being asked to join the army? **Would you fight for your country even if it meant fighting your own family?**

CHAPTER THREE

ALL-OUT WAR

★ ★ ★

Both sides thought it would be a short war. The Confederacy thought its soldiers were better. The Union thought one large battle would decide the war. It marched approximately 35,000 men from Washington, DC, into Virginia.

The Union plan was to cut off the railroad at Manassas, Virginia. The army would then move on to Richmond, the new Confederate capital. About 22,000 Confederate troops moved north from Richmond to meet Union troops.

The battle took place at a river called Bull Run on July 21, 1861. Hundreds of civilians from Washington, DC, went out to watch the battle. Some took a picnic lunch. They expected an easy Union victory.

The Union did well at the beginning of the battle. A Confederate group held a hill. Thomas Jackson led this group. His men stood and fought while others ran. Someone

The First Battle of Bull Run was bloodier than either side expected. ▶

said that Jackson stood like a stone wall, earning him the nickname "Stonewall" Jackson. He inspired the other Confederate soldiers to fight on.

Ten thousand more Confederate troops arrived. In the afternoon, the Confederates launched an attack of their own. This attack sent the Union soldiers retreating back to Washington. The hard-fought battle proved that it would be a long war.

BLACKS FIGHTING IN THE WAR

The 54th Massachusetts was the first **regiment** primarily made up of free Northern blacks to fight in the war. In 1863, the 600 men in the regiment charged Fort Wagner, South Carolina. Nearly half of them were killed, wounded, or missing. By the end of the war, almost 200,000 black Americans served in the Union Army and Navy. They fought bravely for their country, but they were not allowed to be citizens of the United States because of their skin color.

The two sides continued fighting over the next year. Each side won and lost battles. In 1862, Union General Ulysses S. Grant led his army through Tennessee. In April, Grant and his army moved close to the Mississippi border. He thought the Confederates were waiting for Grant to attack them.

Grant was wrong. The Confederates attacked before Grant could. The surprise worked. On the morning of April 6, the Confederates rushed out of the woods near a meeting house called Shiloh.

The battle was on. Fierce advances by the Confederates drove the Union forces backward.

The battle continued the next day. This time the Union army surprised the Confederates by attacking early. The exhausted Confederates withdrew. The battle resulted in nearly 24,000 dead, wounded, or missing soldiers. The large number of **casualties** shocked people in both the North and the South.

Ulysses S. Grant

Both sides claimed victory after the Battle of Shiloh, but it was a failure for the Confederates.

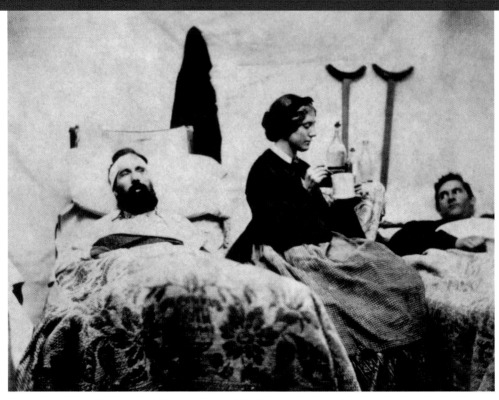
Some women served as nurses and cared for wounded soldiers during the war.

With their husbands at war, many women were left to manage without them. They ran stores and plantations, cared for the kids, or found other work. In both the North and the South, families feared their husbands, brothers, and fathers might never return.

With so much fighting in the South, many women there had to leave their homes to find safer places. Often when they returned, their homes were badly damaged.

Most of the Civil War battles took place in the South. Confederate General Robert E. Lee wanted to take the fight to the Northern states. He invaded Maryland.

Lee's army marched to Sharpsburg. They stopped on high ground near Antietam Creek. On the morning of September 17, 1862, the Union army attacked. It crossed a cornfield. The Confederates were hiding in trees and behind a fence.

Bullets cut through the corn. Union men fell by the dozens. More men kept moving forward. They reached the fence. The Confederates pushed them back. The Confederates then attacked across the same cornfield. Intense fire from the Union hit them. Thousands of men were killed or wounded in that cornfield.

ANOTHER VIEW

The Union and Confederacy both required men to join the army. This was called the draft. In the North, a man could pay $300 to get out of the draft. Many people could not afford this. People in New York City and elsewhere protested with violence. Do you think it was right that rich men could get out of the draft while poorer men could not?

President Lincoln (center) visited Antietam after the Civil War's deadliest battle.

Antietam was the bloodiest day of the war so far. More than 23,000 were killed, wounded, or missing between the two armies. The Union stopped Lee's invasion of the North. But Lee was able to get away.

Five days after the Battle of Antietam, Lincoln issued the **Emancipation** Proclamation. It said that if the Confederacy did not rejoin the Union by January 1, 1863, slaves in areas controlled by the Confederacy would be free. For the North, the war now had a higher purpose.

DISEASE

Battles were not the only dangers soldiers faced. Disease killed two soldiers for every one killed in battle. Dirty camps, a bad diet, and living in close quarters with lots of other soldiers contributed to high levels of sickness.

Confederates used the Mississippi River to ship their supplies. General Grant knew if he captured Vicksburg, Mississippi, the Union would control the Mississippi River.

In May 1863, Grant's army neared the city. The army tried a few attacks. The Confederates beat the attacks back.

Grant then surrounded Vicksburg. His army of approximately 75,000 kept supplies and food from reaching the city. Grant's soldiers also kept firing on the city.

Terrified citizens dug caves to escape the firing. The people were starving. The city was badly damaged. Vicksburg finally surrendered on July 4. The entire Mississippi River now was under Union control. July 4, 1863, would turn out to be an important date in another battle in the North.

CHAPTER FOUR

UNION VICTORIES

★ ★ ★

The Confederates had just won a great victory at Chancellorsville, Virginia. The victory made General Lee bold. He decided to invade Northern territory again. Throughout May and June 1863, Lee's army marched north through Maryland and into Pennsylvania.

Union soldiers also marched north. The two armies met north of Gettysburg, Pennsylvania. On July 1, the battle began. The Confederate army drove the Union army south through the town. The Union forces took up positions on top of Cemetery Hill. After an all-night march, more Union forces arrived for the battle's second day.

Robert E. Lee

Lee thought that the Union army did not have enough men to stop an attack. But the Union fought back all of the Confederates' charges. The Union still held Cemetery Hill.

On July 3, Lee decided to send thousands of men on a charge toward the hill. The Union men had good positions on the hill behind walls. Fewer than half of the Confederates survived. The Confederate army retreated back to Virginia on July 4.

The number of casualties from the three-day battle was shocking. Altogether, approximately 51,000 were killed or wounded. That is nearly one-third of all soldiers who fought in the battle.

Lincoln's (circled) famous Gettysburg Address lasted less than two minutes and was only 272 words long.

Residents lived in constant fear. The Confederate army finally left and the Union army moved in on September 2.

Lincoln was now running for reelection. Other candidates running for president wanted peace talks with the South. The victory in Atlanta made peace talks seem unnecessary.

Sherman's "March to the Sea" resulted in tens of millions of dollars worth of damage to Georgia.

Victory was now clearly in sight for the North. On November 8, Lincoln won the election easily.

Sherman's strategy was now to terrify Southerners. Sherman's army burned Atlanta's factories where guns were made. The fire spread and left the city in ruins.

Sherman's army then marched from Atlanta to the Atlantic Ocean. On the way, Union soldiers raided farms. They took crops and food from homes. They burned barns. Sherman got to Savannah, Georgia, in December. His troops burned property and took food from Southerners in the Carolinas, too.

In the North, Lee's army in Virginia was near total defeat. Lee asked to meet with Union General Grant. People now sensed the war would soon be over.

PRISONERS OF WAR

Prison camps could be just as deadly as battles. Captured soldiers lacked enough food and water. Often, human waste covered the ground. Thousands died from disease. More than 50,000 men died in prison camps on both sides. Neither side had been ready to house that many people for so long.

CHAPTER FIVE

THE END OF THE WAR

Grant and Lee met on April 9, 1865, at Appomattox Court House, Virginia. Lee agreed to Grant's terms of surrender. Lee's men had to lay down their guns. The meeting finally ended the Civil War.

A few days after the Confederates surrendered, Confederate sympathizer John Wilkes Booth shot President Lincoln at a theater in Washington, DC. Lincoln died the next morning on April 14, 1865. But he had won the war.

In total, more than 620,000 people were killed in the Civil War. The entire country was shaken. But the Union stayed together despite its wounds.

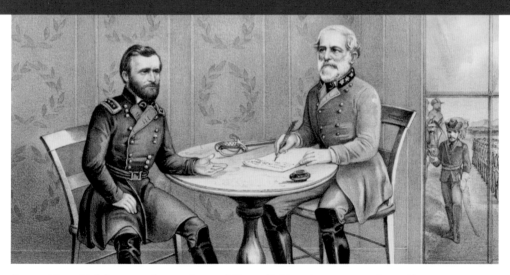

General Lee (right) surrenders to General Grant (left) at Appomattox Court House on April 9, 1865.

A series of new laws gave former slaves their freedom. The 13th, 14th, and 15th Amendments to the U.S. Constitution abolished slavery, gave blacks equality under the law, and guaranteed their right to vote. But blacks would continue to be treated unfairly for years to come.

Imagine you are either General Lee or General Grant. You are about to meet face-to-face after the long, terrible war. What would you say to the other general?

TIMELINE

1859	John Brown raids Harpers Ferry.
December 20, 1860	South Carolina secedes from the Union.
April 12, 1861	Confederate cannons fire on Fort Sumter, South Carolina.
July 21, 1861	The first battle of the Civil War takes place near Manassas, Virginia.
September 22, 1862	Abraham Lincoln issues the Emancipation Proclamation, to take effect on January 1, 1863.
July 4, 1863	Confederate forces surrender Vicksburg, Mississippi.
July 4, 1863	Union forces win a key battle at Gettysburg, Pennsylvania.
November 19, 1863	President Lincoln presents the Gettysburg Address.
September 2, 1864	Union General Sherman takes Atlanta.
November 8, 1864	Lincoln wins reelection.
April 9, 1865	General Lee surrenders to General Grant at Appomattox Court House, Virginia.
April 15, 1865	Lincoln dies after being shot in the head by John Wilkes Booth the previous night.

GLOSSARY

abolish (uh-BAH-lish) To abolish something is to put an end to it officially. Many people in the North wanted to abolish slavery before the Civil War.

abolitionist (ab-uh-LISH-uh-nist) An abolitionist was someone who worked to abolish slavery before the Civil War. John Brown became a famous abolitionist after his raid on Harpers Ferry.

armory (AHR-mur-ee) Weapons are stored in an armory. An armory could be a valuable military target.

artillery (ahr-TIL-ur-ee) Large, powerful guns that are mounted on wheels are called artillery. The soldiers who use these weapons can also be called the artillery.

casualties (KAZH-oo-uhl-teez) Casualties are soldiers who are wounded, captured, missing, or killed in war. Casualties include more than just those soldiers who are killed.

draft (DRAFT) The draft required men of a certain age in the United States and the Confederate States to join the military. A Union man could get out of the draft during the Civil War by paying $300 or by hiring someone else to take his place.

emancipation (i-man-suh-PAY-shun) Emancipation is the freeing of people from slavery. President Lincoln ordered the emancipation of Confederate slaves in 1863.

infantry (IN-fun-tree) The foot soldiers of an army are called the infantry. The infantry did most of the fighting in the Civil War.

plantations (plan-TAY-shuns) Plantations are large farms common in the South before the Civil War. A plantation usually employed many slaves.

regiment (REJ-uh-munt) A regiment is a group of soldiers. A regiment in the Civil War was usually made up of soldiers from the same state.

seceded (si-SEE-did) States that have seceded no longer want to be part of a country. Southern states seceded from the United States after Abraham Lincoln was elected president.

siege (seej) A siege is the surrounding of a place to stop supplies from entering. A siege can be very hard for civilians in the city.

TO LEARN MORE

BOOKS

The Civil War Trust. *The Civil War Kids 150: Fifty Fun Things to Do, See, Make, and Find for the 150th Anniversary.* Guilford, CT: Globe Pequot Press, 2012.

Stanchak, John. *Eyewitness Civil War.* New York: DK Publishing, 2011.

Yancey, Diane. *Life in the South during the Civil War.* San Diego: ReferencePoint Press, 2014.

WEB SITES

Visit our Web site for links about the Civil War: **childsworld.com/links**

Note to Parents, Teachers, and Librarians: We routinely verify our Web links to make sure they are safe and active sites. So encourage your readers to check them out!

INDEX